Oh! What a Surprise!

Suzanne Bloom

BOYDS MILLS PRESS
AN IMPRINT OF BOYDS MILLS & KANE
New York

To Fred, who always finds the best surprises

Boyds Mills Press
An imprint of Boyds Mills & Kane,
a division of Astra Publishing House
boydsmillspress.com

Printed in China

ISBN: 978-1-59078 -892-9 (hardcover)
ISBN: 978-1-63592-301-8 (pb)
Library of Congress Control Number: 2012933453

First paperback edition, 2020
10 9 8 7 6 5 4 3 2 1

The text for this book is set in
ITC Legacy Sans Medium.
The illustrations are done in pastel.

What are you doing?
Are you making something?

It's a surprise.

I love surprises!
Can I see?
Can I help?
Is it for me?

If it's for me, it's too long!

It's not for you.

Oh. That's OK.

Is it for Goose?
Goose doesn't like surprises.
Besides, Goose is busy.

Goose is making something.
Maybe that's for me.
I'll go see.

Oh Goosey...
What are you doing?
Are you making a surprise?
Can I see?
Is it for Bear?
Is it for me?

If it's for me, it's too big.

It’s not for you.

Oh. That's OK.

But I love surprises.

I know.
I will make my own surprise.
Something spectacular.
I will wrap it up
and it will be so beautiful.

It’s time for surprises.

Me first! Open me first!

Ta da!
It's me. For you!

What a surprise.
A splendid surprise!

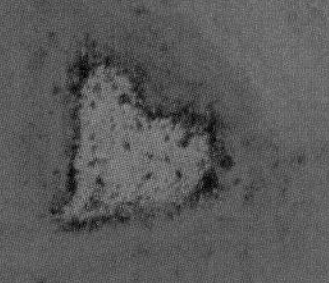

We made something for you, too.

For me? Really?

I love surprises!

Let's do it again!